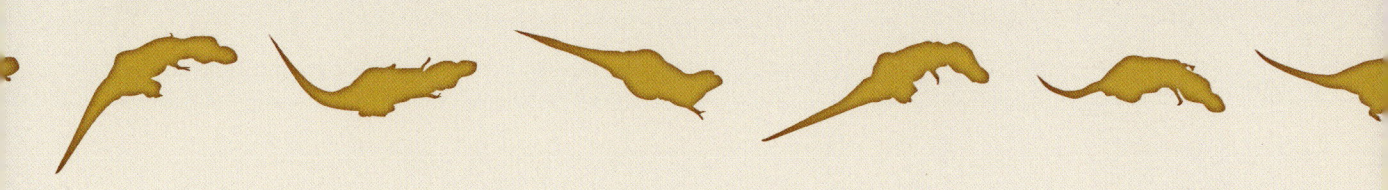

The Age of Dinosaurs

Meet Diplodocus

Written by Sheryn Knight

Illustrations by Leonello Calvetti and Luca Massini

Cavendish Square

New York

Published in 2015 by Cavendish Square Publishing, LLC
243 5th Avenue, Suite 136, New York, NY 10016

Copyright © 2015 by Cavendish Square Publishing, LLC

First Edition

No part of this publication may be reproduced, stored in a retrieval system, or transmitted in any form or by any means—electronic, mechanical, photocopying, recording, or otherwise—without the prior permission of the copyright owner. Request for permission should be addressed to Permissions, Cavendish Square Publishing, 243 5th Avenue, Suite 136, New York, NY 10016. Tel (877) 980-4450; fax (877) 980-4454.

Website: cavendishsq.com

This publication represents the opinions and views of the author based on his or her personal experience, knowledge, and research. The information in this book serves as a general guide only. The author and publisher have used their best efforts in preparing this book and disclaim liability rising directly or indirectly from the use and application of this book.

CPSIA Compliance Information: Batch #WS14CSQ

All websites were available and accurate when this book was sent to press.

Knight, Sheryn, 1967-
Meet Diplodocus / Sheryn Knight.
pages cm. — (The age of dinosaurs)
Includes bibliographical references and index.
ISBN 978-1-62712-782-0 (hardcover) ISBN 978-1-62712-783-7 (paperback) ISBN 978-1-62712-784-4 (ebook)
1. Diplodocus—Juvenile literature. I. Title.

QE862.S3K63 2015
567.913—dc23

2014001523

Editorial Director: Dean Miller
Copy Editor: Cynthia Roby
Art Director: Jeffrey Talbot
Designer: Douglas Brooks
Photo Researcher: J8 Media
Production Manager: Jennifer Ryder-Talbot
Production Editor: David McNamara
Illustrations by Leonello Calvetti and Luca Massini

The photographs in this book are used by permission and through the courtesy of:
Jeffery M. Frank/Shutterstock.com, 8; Anky-man/File:Lance Fm.jpg/Wikimedia Commons, 8; Sam Pierson/Photo Researchers/Getty Images, 20; Universal History Archive/Universal Images Group/Getty Images, 21.

Printed in the United States of America

CONTENTS

1	A CHANGING WORLD	4
2	A LONG-NECKED DINOSAUR	6
3	FINDING DIPLODOCUS	8
4	YOUNG DIPLODOCUS	10
5	MIGRATION	13
6	DINING WITH DIPLODOCUS	14
7	TRAPPED	16
8	INSIDE DIPLODOCUS	18
9	UNEARTHING DIPLODOCUS	20
10	THE DIPLODOCIDS	22
11	THE GREAT EXTINCTION	24
12	A DINOSAUR'S FAMILY TREE	26
	A SHORT VOCABULARY OF DINOSAURS	28
	DINOSAUR WEBSITES	30
	MUSEUMS	31
	INDEX	32

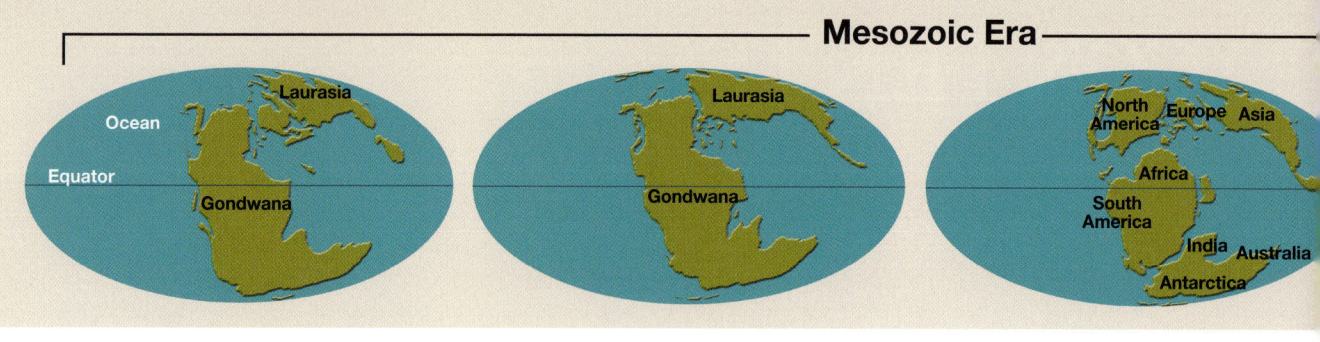

Mesozoic Era

Late Triassic
227 – 206 million years ago.

Early Jurassic
206 –176 million years ago.

Middle Jurassic
176 – 159 million years ago.

A CHANGING WORLD

Dinosaurs roamed the Earth many years before humans even existed. The world of the dinosaurs was very different from the world of today. To understand the dinosaur world, you need to know more about the history of the Earth.

Earth has been around for 4.6 billion years. Geologists and archeologists use special terms to understand geological time. They group periods of time into eras, periods, epochs, and ages. Dinosaurs lived during the Mesozoic era. The Mesozoic era is divided into three periods: the Triassic period, which lasted 42

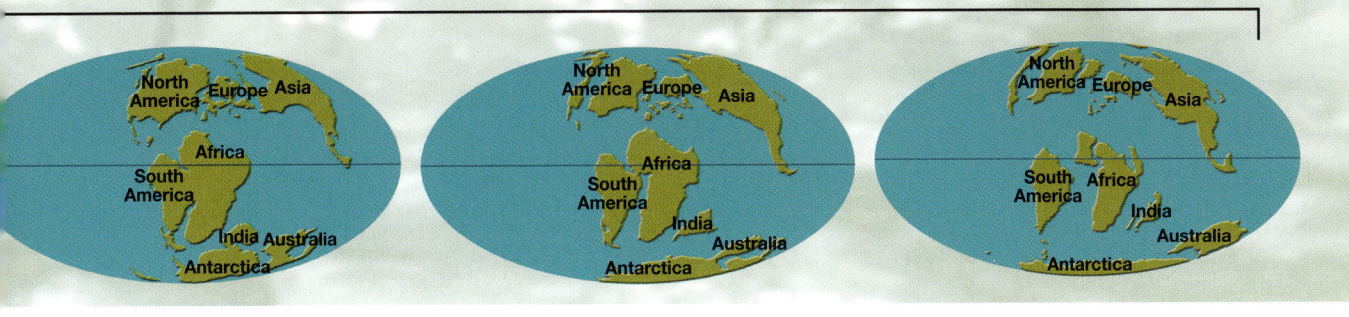

Late Jurassic
159 – 144 million years ago.

Early Cretaceous
144 – 99 million years ago.

Late Cretaceous
99 – 65 million years ago.

million years; the Jurassic period, which lasted 61 million years; and the Cretaceous period, which lasted 79 million years.

Dinosaurs ruled the world for over 160 million years, but they became extinct nearly 65 million years before the first person walked the Earth.

A LONG-NECKED DINOSAUR

Diplodocus (pronounced dip-LOW-doe-kuss) was a Saurischian dinosaur belonging to the order *Saurischia*, meaning "lizard-hipped," and the suborder *Sauropoda*, meaning "lizard-footed." These orders roamed Earth between the Late Triassic and the end of the Cretaceous periods between 65 and 203 million years ago.

The name Diplodocus comes from the Greek and means "double beam." This refers to the shape of its chevrons, the small bones along the lower side of the dinosaur's tail. American paleontologist Othniel Charles Marsh gave Diplodocus its name in 1878.

In measuring Diplodocus' complete skeleton, paleontologists concluded that it was the longest dinosaur known. Its average length was about 90 feet (27 meters), although an adult Diplodocus could measure up to 175 feet (53 m). Its neck measured 26 feet (8 m) long and its tail was 45 feet (14 m) long. Paleontologists believe that Diplodocus may have used its tail like a whip to scare off predators, although other dinosaurs were likely intimidated by its size.

Paleontologist once thought that Diplodocus's nostrils were on top of its head. However, a recent discovery proves that its nostrils were located on either side of the dinosaur's mouth. The dinosaur had about 40 pencil-shaped teeth, all of which pointed forward.

FINDING DIPLODOCUS

Diplodocus roamed the Earth during the Late Jurassic period, some 148 to 155 million years ago, in North America. Because of its size, Diplodocus lived in more open environments. Traveling in herds, it roamed along the rivers, lakes, and vast plains of an area known today as the Rocky Mountain region of Colorado, Montana, Utah, and Wyoming.

Paleontologists recognize four species of Diplodocus: *Diplodocus longus* (the first of the species discovered), *D. carnegiei*, *D. hay*, and *D. lacustris*.

Montana

Wyoming

NORTH AMERICA

This map shows western North America in the Late Jurassic period. The dark brown area indicates mountains, and the red dots Diplodocus fossil discovery sites.

YOUNG DIPLODOCUS

Paleontologists hypothesized that Diplodocus did not build nests or make other preparations for their young. Instead they laid eggs while walking. The female Diplodocus laid large sphere-shaped eggs and covered them with vegetation. When the egg hatched, baby Diplodocus was about 3.3 feet (1 m) long, with a large head, a short snout, and enormous eyes. Early on, Diplodocus grew rapidly. After about ten years, it grew slowly for the rest of its life.

II

12

MIGRATION

There were dry seasons in the Rocky Mountain regions where Diplodocus roamed. During these times, paleontologists believe that Diplodocus migrated to more humid zones. The dinosaur was then able to find enough food in the lusher feeding grounds.

The dinosaurs stuck together in herds during these migrations. Predatory dinosaurs, such as the Allosaurus, followed the herds. If they found a straggler that could not keep up with the herd, it would become an easy victim.

DINING WITH DIPLODOCUS

Diplodocus's thin teeth were located only in the front part of its jaws, so paleontologists consider the dinosaur an herbivore, feeding mostly on plants. Its teeth were used to strip leaves from branches. Since its long neck was able to move about in every direction, the dinosaur could reach food both close to the ground and high up in the trees. Diplodocus did not chew the leaves, but swallowed them whole.

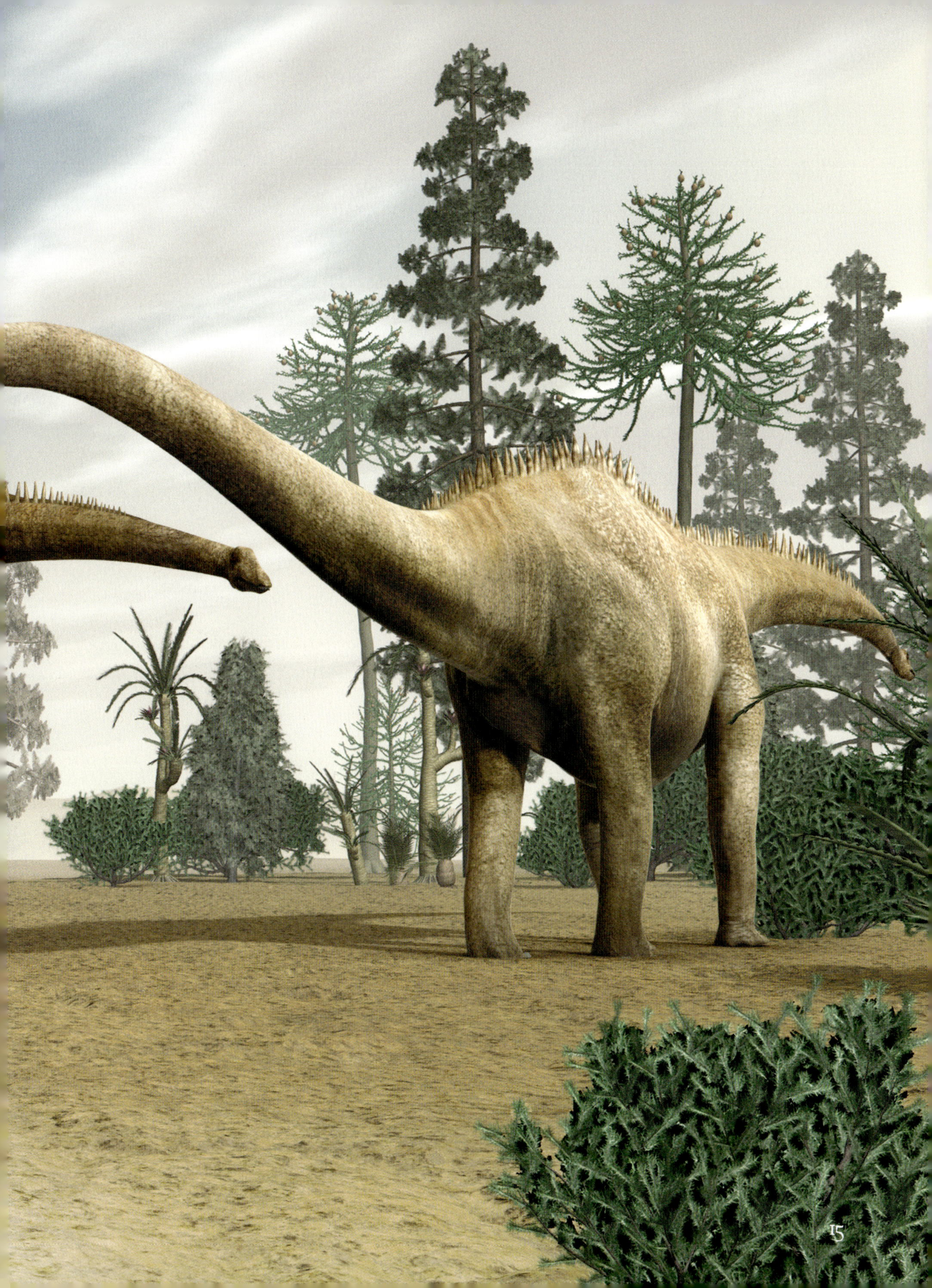

TRAPPED

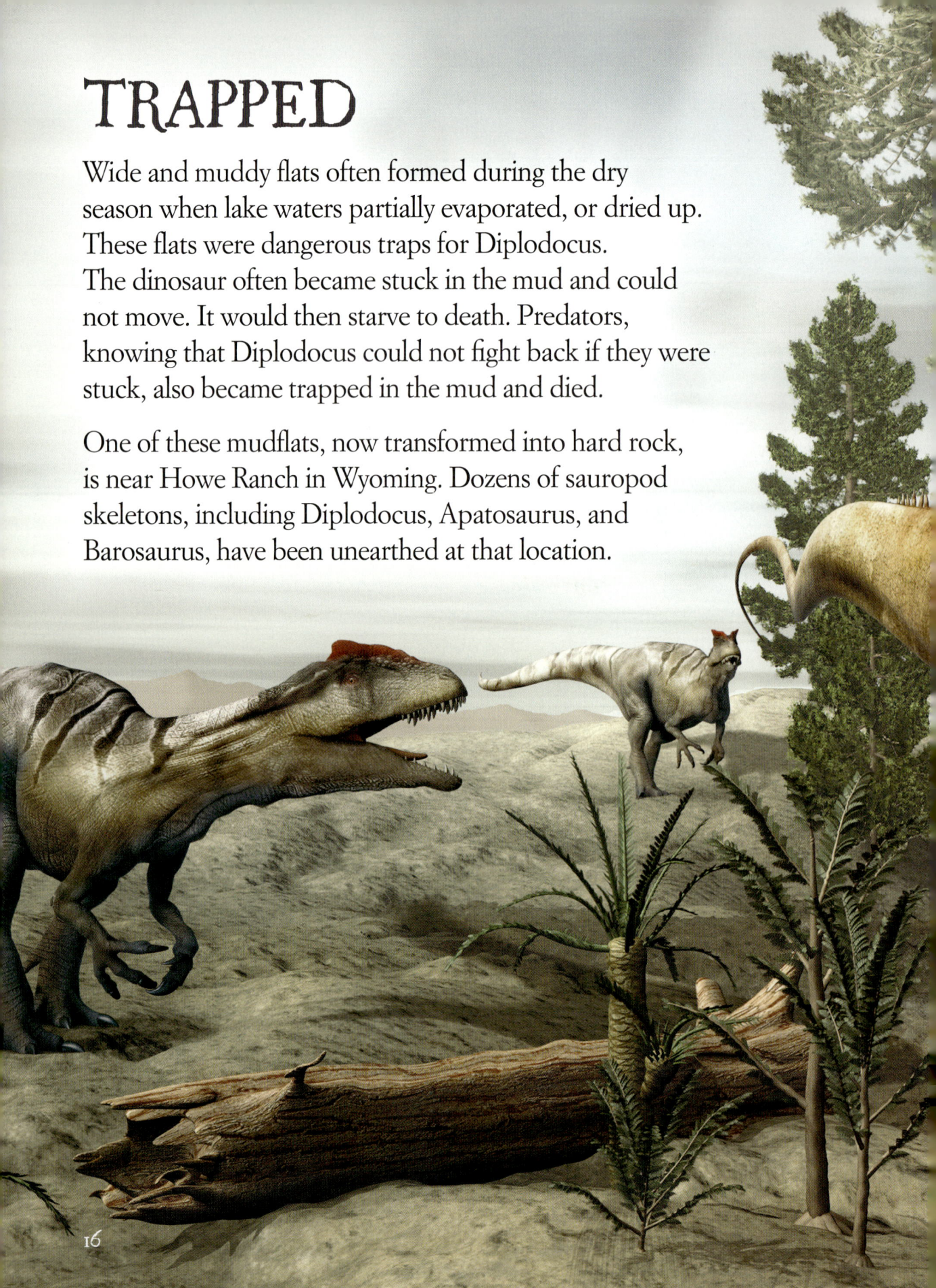

Wide and muddy flats often formed during the dry season when lake waters partially evaporated, or dried up. These flats were dangerous traps for Diplodocus. The dinosaur often became stuck in the mud and could not move. It would then starve to death. Predators, knowing that Diplodocus could not fight back if they were stuck, also became trapped in the mud and died.

One of these mudflats, now transformed into hard rock, is near Howe Ranch in Wyoming. Dozens of sauropod skeletons, including Diplodocus, Apatosaurus, and Barosaurus, have been unearthed at that location.

17

INSIDE DIPLODOCUS

Paleontologists consider Diplodocus to have been a lightweight dinosaur because its massive body weighed only about 12 tons (11,000 kilograms). The dinosaur's head measured less than 2 feet (60 centimeters) long. One toe on each of its five-toed feet had a thumb claw, most likely for self-defense. Because Diplodocus's front legs were shorter than its back legs, it was one of the slower-moving dinosaurs at only about 5 to 9 miles per hour (8 to 15 km per hour).

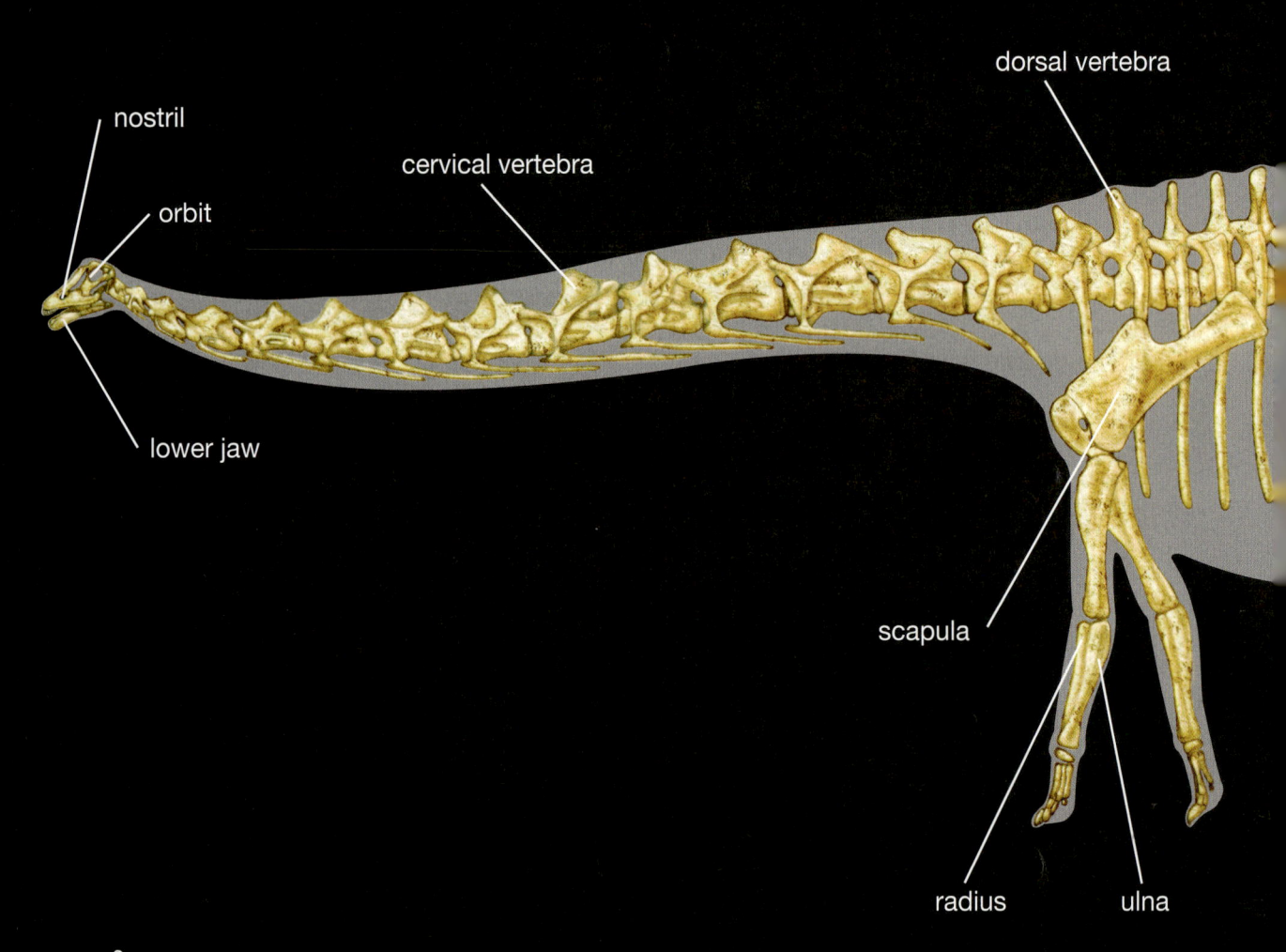

Forefoot bones with the lateral claw

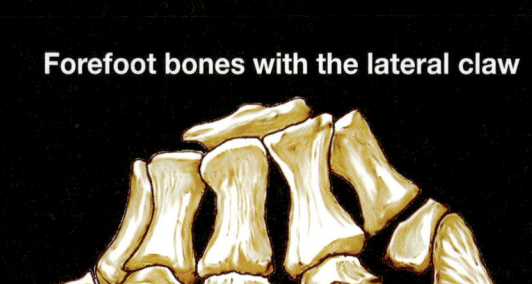

Hind foot bones with two claws

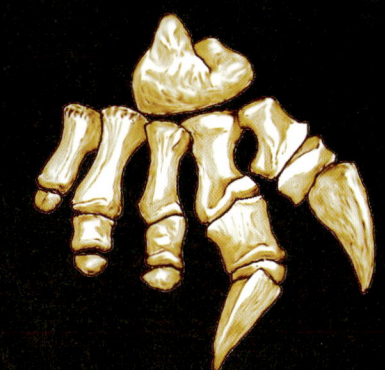

Dorsal view of the skull

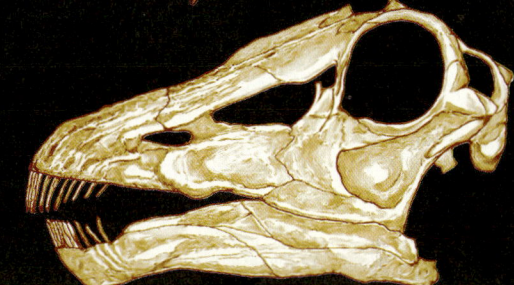

Side view of the skull

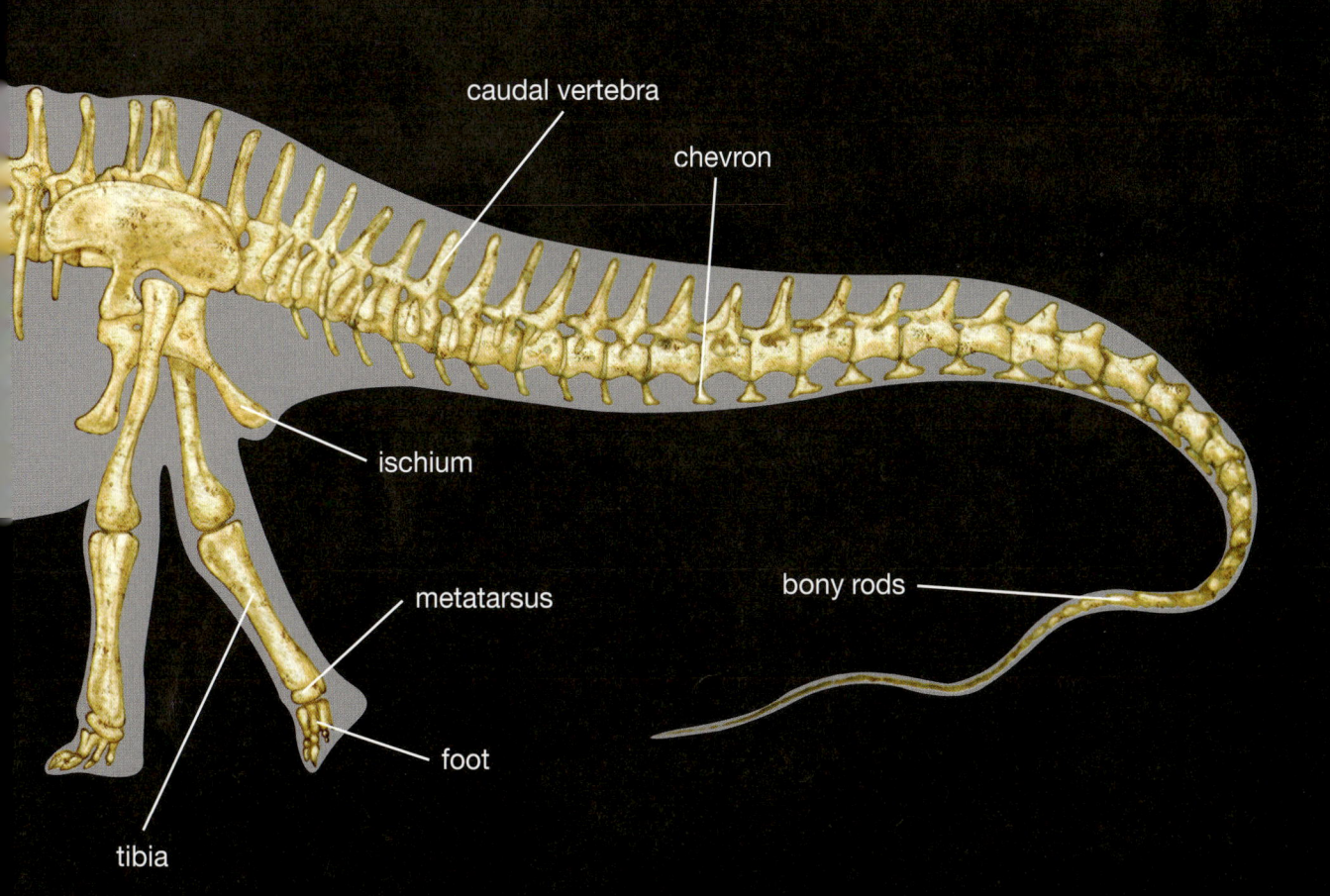

- caudal vertebra
- chevron
- ischium
- metatarsus
- bony rods
- foot
- tibia

UNEARTHING DIPLODOCUS

The first Diplodocus fossil was unearthed in 1877 at Dinosaur Ridge in Morrison, Colorado, by fossil hunters Earl Douglass and Samuel W. Williston. The most complete Diplodocus fossil was unearthed in 1899 from the Morrison Formation of Sheep Creek, Wyoming, a Late Jurassic sedimentary rock sequence. A number of Diplodocus fossils have since been found in the Rocky Mountain region of Colorado, Montana, Utah, and Wyoming.

A Diplodocus skeleton on display at the Museum of Natural History in Houston, Texas.

A paleontologist unearths the massive hind leg of a Diplodocus.

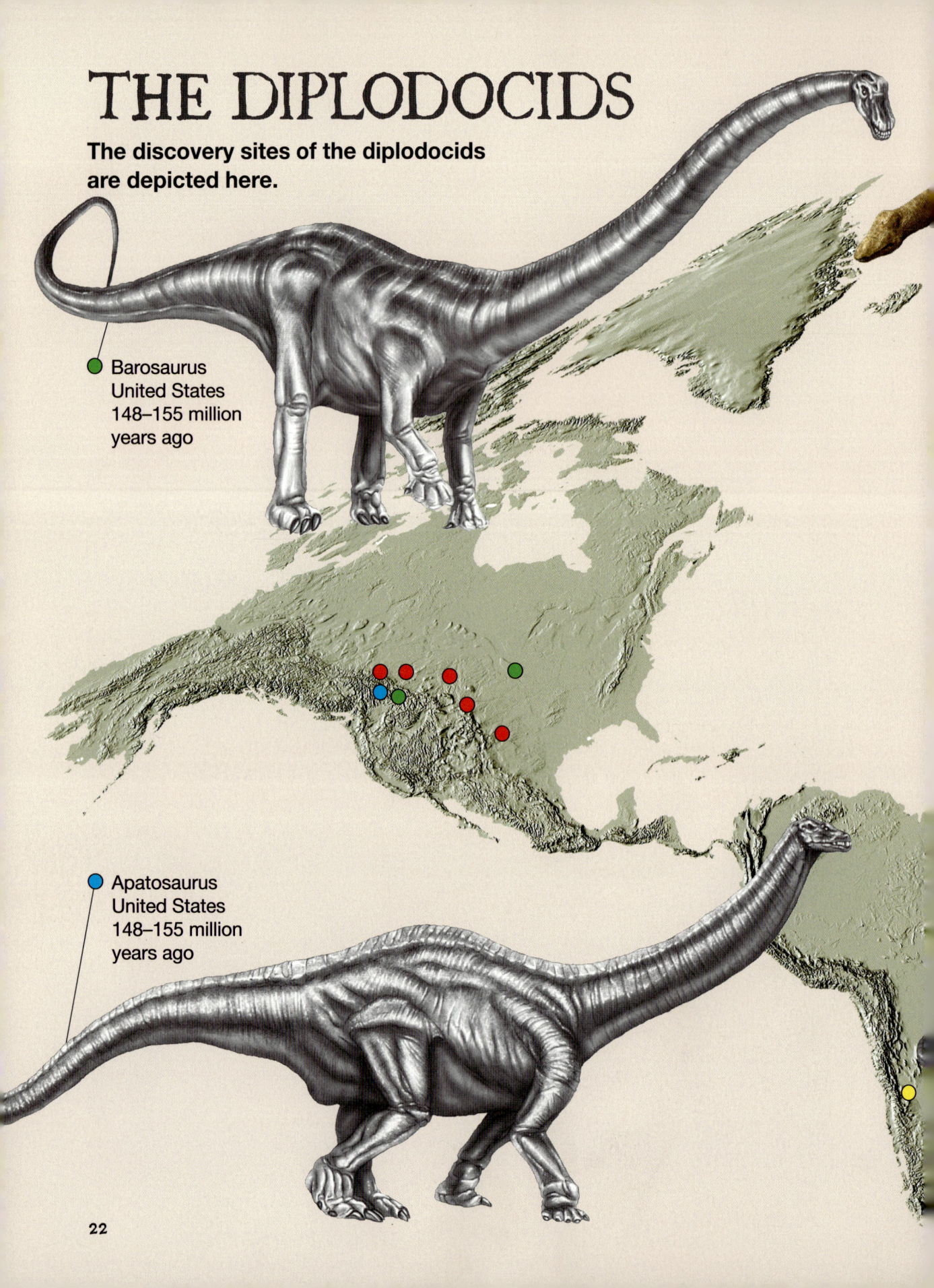

THE DIPLODOCIDS

The discovery sites of the diplodocids are depicted here.

● Barosaurus
United States
148–155 million
years ago

● Apatosaurus
United States
148–155 million
years ago

22

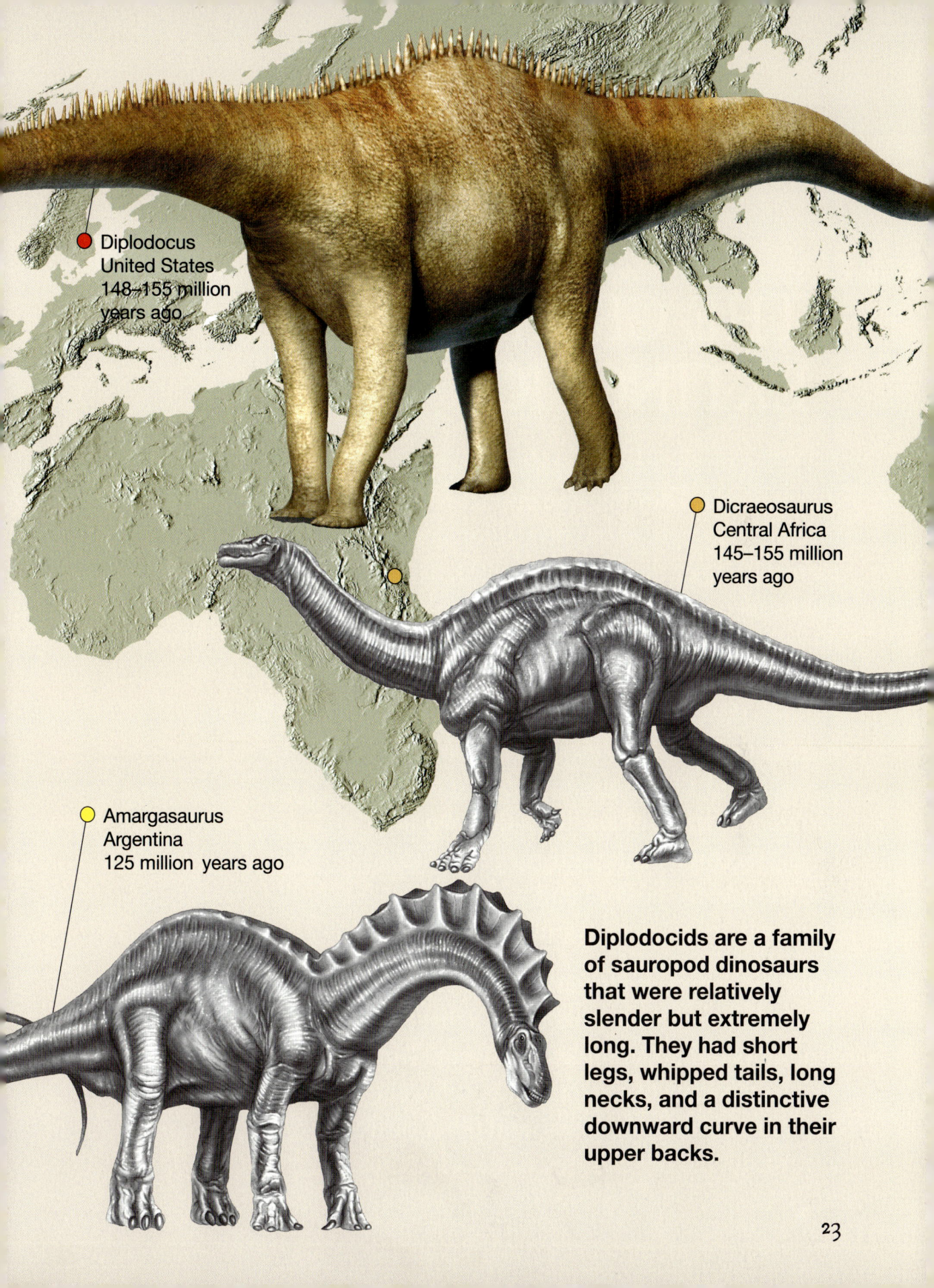

● Diplodocus
United States
148–155 million
years ago

● Dicraeosaurus
Central Africa
145–155 million
years ago

● Amargasaurus
Argentina
125 million years ago

Diplodocids are a family of sauropod dinosaurs that were relatively slender but extremely long. They had short legs, whipped tails, long necks, and a distinctive downward curve in their upper backs.

23

THE GREAT EXTINCTION

It's still a mystery how the dinosaurs disappeared. They became extinct 65 million years ago, about 80 million years after the age of the Diplodocus. Many scientists believe that this was caused by a meteorite hitting the Earth. A large crater about 65 million years old was discovered close to the coast of Mexico. If a large meteor hit the Earth, the impact would have caused a huge amount of dust to enter the Earth's atmosphere. This dust would have prevented sunlight from getting to the surface. In the cold and without the sunshine, many plants would have died.

Most dinosaurs either starved or froze to death. However, scientists believe that the dinosaurs did not completely die out. Today, the descendants of the dinosaurs still walk the Earth. Chickens, crows, and other birds are considered the children of the dinosaurs.

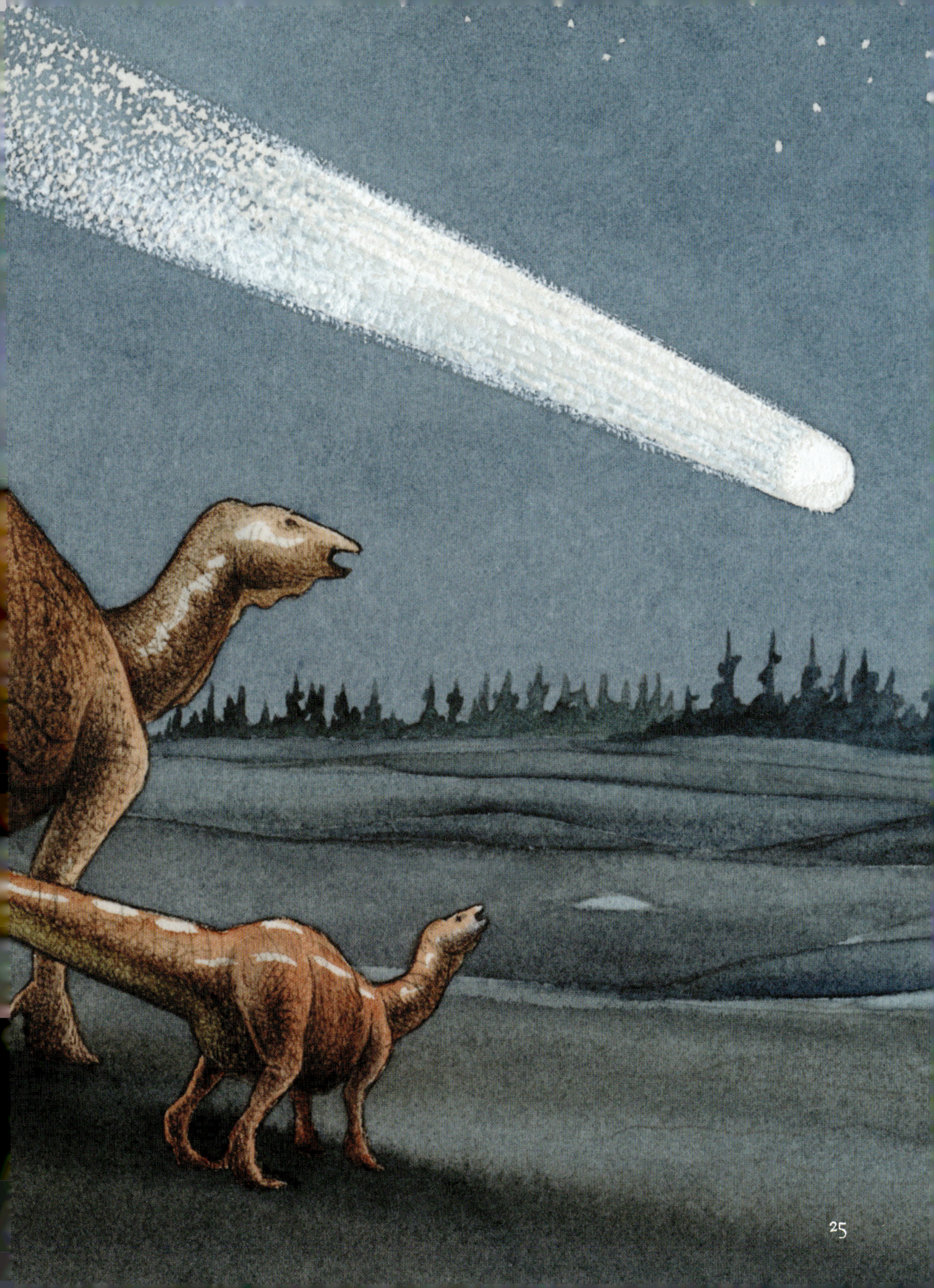

A DINOSAUR'S FAMILY TREE

The oldest dinosaur fossils are 220–225 million years old and have been found all over the world.

Dinosaurs are divided into two groups. Saurischians are similar to reptiles, with the pubic bone directed forward, while the Ornithischians are like birds, with the pubic bone directed backward.

Saurischians are subdivided in two main groups: Sauropodomorphs, to which quadrupeds and vegetarians belong; and Theropods, which include bipeds and predators.

Ornithischians are subdivided into three large groups: Thyreophorans, which include the quadrupeds Stegosaurians and Ankylosaurians; Ornithopods; and Marginocephalians, which are subdivided into the bipedal Pachycephalosaurians and the mainly quadrupedal Ceratopsians.

26

Triceratops •   *Ornithomimus* •   *Tyrannosaurus*   *Velociraptor* •

Pachycephalosaurus

Giganotosaurus •

Ceratopsians

Ornithomimids

Tyrannosauroids

Oviraptorosaurians

Deinonychosaurians

Birds

Scipionyx •

Deinonychus •

Caudipteryx •

Sauropods

Ornitholeste

Brachiosaurus •

Diplodocus •

Marginocephalians

Theropods

Plateosaurus •

Prosauropods

Sauropodomorphs

Saurischians

Dinosauria

27

A SHORT VOCABULARY OF DINOSAURS

Bipedal: pertaining to an animal moving on two feet alone, almost always those of the hind legs.

Bone: hard tissue made mainly of calcium phosphate; single element of the skeleton.

Carnivore: a meat-eating animal.

Caudal: pertaining to the tail.

Cenozoic Era (Caenozoic, Tertiary Era): the interval of geological time between 65 million years ago and present day.

Cervical: pertaining to the neck.

Claws: the fingers and toes of predator animals end with pointed and sharp nails, called claws. Those of plant-eaters end with blunt nails, called hooves.

Cretaceous Period: the interval of geological time between 144 and 65 million years ago.

Egg: a large cell enclosed in a porous shell produced by reptiles and birds to reproduce themselves.

Epoch: a memorable date or event.

Evolution: changes in the character states of organisms, species, and higher ranks through time.

Extinct: when something, such as a species of animal, is no longer existing.

Feathers: outgrowth of the skin of birds and some dinosaurs, used in flight and in providing insulation and protection for the body. They evolved from reptilian scales.

Forage: to wander in search of food.

Fossil: evidence of life in the past. Not only bones, but footprints and trails made by animals, as well as dung, eggs or plant resin, when fossilized, are fossils.

Herbivore: a plant-eating animal.

Jurassic Period: the interval of geological time between 206 and 144 million years ago.

Mesozoic Era (Mesozoic, Secondary Era): the interval of geological time between 248 and 65 million years ago.

Pack: a group of predator animals acting together to capture their prey.

Paleontologist: a scientist who studies and reconstructs the prehistoric life.

Paleozoic Era (Paleozoic, Primary Era): the interval of geological time between 570 and 248 million years ago.

Predator: an animal that preys on other animals for food.

Raptor (raptorial): a bird of prey, such as an eagle, hawk, falcon, or owl.

Rectrix (plural rectrices): any of the larger feathers in a bird's tail that are important in helping its flight direction.

Scavenger: an animal that eats dead animals.

Skeleton: a structure of an animal's body made of several different bones. One primary function is to protect delicate organs such as the brain, lungs, and heart.

Skin: the external, thin layer of the animal body. Skin cannot fossilize, unless it is covered by scales, feathers, or fur.

Skull: bones that protect the brain and the face.

Teeth: tough structures in the jaws used to hold, cut, and sometimes process food.

Terrestrial: living on land.

Triassic Period: the interval of geological time between 248 and 206 million years ago.

Unearth: to find something that was buried beneath the earth.

Vertebrae: the single bones of the backbone; they protect the spinal cord.

DINOSAUR WEBSITES

Dino Database
www.dinodatabase.com
Get the latest news on dinosaur research and discoveries. This site is pretty advanced, so you may need help from a teacher or parent to find what you're looking for.

Dinosaurs for Kids
www.kidsdinos.com
There's basic information about most dinosaur types, and you can play dinosaur games, vote for your favorite dinosaur, and learn about the study of dinosaurs, paleontology.

Dinosaur Train
pbskids.org/dinosaurtrain
From the PBS show *Dinosaur Train*, you can watch videos, print out pages to color, play games, and learn lots of facts about so many dinosaurs!

Discovery Channel Dinosaur Videos
discovery.com/video-topics/other/other-topics-dinosaur-videos.htm
Watch almost 100 videos about the life of dinosaurs!

The Natural History Museum
www.nhm.ac.uk/kids-only/dinosaurs
Take a quiz to see how much you know about dinosaurs—or a quiz to tell you what type of dinosaur you'd be! There's also a fun directory of dinosaurs, including some cool 3-D views of your favorites.

MUSEUMS

American Museum of Natural History, New York, NY
www.amnh.org

Carnegie Museum of Natural History, Pittsburgh, PA
www.carnegiemnh.org

Denver Museum of Nature and Science, Denver, CO
www.dmns.org

Dinosaur National Monument, Dinosaur, CO
www.nps.gov/dino

The Field Museum, Chicago, IL
fieldmuseum.org

University of California Museum of Paleontology, Berkeley, CA
www.ucmp.berkeley.edu

Museum of the Rockies, Bozeman, MT
www.museumoftherockies.org

National Museum of Natural History, Smithsonian Institution, Washington, DC
www.mnh.si.edu

Royal Tyrrell Museum of Palaeontology, Drumheller, Canada
www.tyrrellmuseum.com

Sam Noble Museum of Natural History, Norman, OK
www.snomnh.ou.edu

Yale Peabody Museum of Natural History, New Haven, CT
peabody.yale.edu

INDEX

Page numbers in **boldface** are illustrations.

Cretaceous period, **5**, 6, **26–27**

Diplodocus
   size, 6–7, 10,
   where discovered, 8, **9**, 16, 20, **22–23**
   young, 10
Douglass, Earl, 20

epoch, 4

food, 13, 14
fossil, **9**, **18–19**, 20, 26

herbivore, 14

Jurassic period, **4–5**, 8, **9**, 20, **26–27**

Marsh, Othniel Charles, 6
Mesozoic era, **4–5**
mudflats, 16

paleontologist, 6, 7, 8, 10, 13, 14, 18, **21**

Saurischian, 6, 26, **27**
skeleton, 6, 16, **18–19**, **21**
skull, 18, **19**

teeth, 7, 14
Triassic period, **4**, 6, **26–27**

Williston, Samuel W., 20